UNDEAD PETS

GOLDFISH FROM BEYOND THE GRAVE

For Alice and Archie – SH

For lovely little Lily – SC

STRIPES PUBLISHING
An imprint of Little Tiger Press
1 The Coda Centre, 189 Munster Road,
London SW6 6AW

A paperback original
First published in Great Britain in 2013

Text copyright © Sam Hay, 2013
Illustrations copyright © Simon Cooper, 2013

ISBN: 978-1-84715-365-4

A CIP catalogue record for this book is available from
the British Library.

Printed and bound in the UK.
10 9 8 7 6 5 4 3 2 1

UNDEAD PETS

GOLDFISH FROM BEYOND THE GRAVE

SAM HAY

ILLUSTRATED BY SIMON COOPER

Stripes

The story so far...

Ten-year-old Joe Edmunds is desperate for a pet.

But his mum's allergies mean that he's got no chance.

Then his great-uncle Charlie gives him an ancient Egyptian amulet that he claims will grant Joe a single wish...

But instead of getting a pet, Joe becomes the Protector of Undead Pets. He is bound by the amulet to solve the problems of zombie pets so they can pass peacefully to the afterlife.

CHAPTER ONE

"Three… Two… One… Go!"

Joe shot away from the side of the swimming pool, like a great white shark on the attack. He swam out of the deep end, arms cutting through the water, pausing just for a second to glance back. "Come on, Matt, what's keeping you?"

His best mate's head bobbed up next to him. "What's keeping *you*, you mean!" And he hurtled past Joe, kicking water in his face.

Joe spat out a mouthful and raced after him.

"I'm on your tail," he yelled. He dodged past two old grannies doing lengths, and a couple of smaller kids practising their breaststroke. But Matt was already halfway down the pool. Joe stuck his face in the water and raced on. He was gaining on Matt now, with just a few metres to go…

But then something wobbled out in front of him. Joe collided with a small girl in armbands who was doing backstroke.

"Be careful over there!" shouted the lifeguard from the other side of the pool.

"Sorry," muttered Joe. He could see Matt already in the shallows, laughing and punching the air. He'd won!

Joe groaned and swam over.

"What took you so long?" said Matt, grinning.

"Very funny!" said Joe. He gave a cheeky smile. "Actually, Matt, I forgot to tell you, the race was two lengths – not one!"

"What?"

"See ya!" Joe launched into the water and powered back towards the deep end.

"Hey!" Matt began to chase after him, but the swimming grannies were in his way. He dodged round them, and then got tangled up with Joe's dad and Toby, Joe's little brother, who was practising underwater turns.

"Sorry, Mr Edmunds!" Matt called, as he splashed past them. But Joe had already reached the other end of the pool. He was hauling himself up on to the side by the time Matt arrived.

"Loser!" smirked Joe.

"That was such a lame trick!" Matt climbed out of the water next to Joe. They sat, watching the swimmers and swinging their feet in the water.

"Hey, guess what?" Matt said. "My cousin's fish have turned cannibal!"

"What?"

"You know Dan, my older cousin? Well, one of his goldfish has been eaten by another fish."

"No way!"

"One day it was swimming around in the tank with the others, the next it was gone. Swallowed whole…"

"Gross!"

"Dan's gutted. Fizz – the one that got eaten – was his first goldfish. He'd had him since he was little."

"What kind of fish are the other ones? Piranhas or something?" asked Joe.

"Nope, there's one guppy, but apart from that, they're just goldfish!"

"*Killer* goldfish!" Joe grinned.

He was just about to slip back into the water when he spotted something dart past his toes. "Hey, what was that?"

"Mmm?" said Matt.

Joe scanned the water. "I know it sounds crazy, but I think I just saw a fish…"

"You're mad!" Matt gave Joe a shove, and he splashed back into the water, pretending to sink like a stone. Then he bounced off the bottom and shot back up, grabbing Matt's ankles and hauling him into the water, too.

"Race you!" Joe shouted, pushing off and

zooming down the pool.

Matt gave chase, but Joe was ahead … until Toby decided he wanted to join in.

"Hey, Joe," he called, paddling over and grabbing his big brother's arm.

"Watch it!" yelled Joe.

"I win!" Matt called, as he hurtled past him.

"Thanks a lot!" Joe glared at his little brother.

Toby bit his lip. "Sorry, I just wanted to play."

Dad called over to them, "Time to get out now, boys."

"Five more minutes?" begged Joe.

"You can stay in for two more minutes," said Dad. "Come on, Toby, shower time."

"No!" Toby wailed. "That's not fair!"

"Hey, Matt," Joe shouted. "One last race?"

"Sure! First one back to the deep end…" And he raced off.

But just as Joe was about to swim after him, he spotted something streaking through the water. Then he felt something cold and slimy.

Joe peered down. It was a fish – a slightly green goldfish! And it had suckered itself on to his toe.

"Gerr-off!" Joe yelped, trying to flick it away. But the fish held tight. Joe dunked his head into the water and grabbed his foot with both hands, but just as he went to pull the fish away, it let go.

"Hello, Joe," it said, a stream of green bubbles popping out of its mouth. "I've been looking for you."

Joe swallowed a lungful of water in shock. Coughing and spluttering, he bobbed up to the surface. The fish followed, floating next to him.

"Going somewhere?" it said sarcastically.

Joe looked at its single goggly eye and its slimy gills and groaned. It was an undead pet — another zombie creature who needed his help. Ever since Uncle Charlie had given Joe a magical Egyptian amulet, there had been a series of undead animals turning up on his doorstep, unable to pass over to the afterlife until he'd helped them solve their problems.

The fish fixed Joe with a dead-eyed stare. "Listen to me," it said in a raspy voice. "I'm gonna make you an offer you can't refuse. Help me, or else there'll be trouble!"

"Who do you think you are?" spluttered Joe. "You can't order me around like that!"

The fish didn't blink. "Don't mess with me, or you'll regret it."

CHAPTER TWO

Joe couldn't help laughing. Here he was being bullied by a small goldfish — a small, *undead* goldfish! It was ridiculous.

"My name is Fizz," said the fish.

Joe gasped. "What? You're not *Dan's* dead fish, are you?"

"Yeah, and I want you to find out who killed me."

"But that's easy — another fish did. It ate you!"

Fizz puffed up like a balloon. "That's rubbish!"

"It's true! Matt just told me." Just then, Joe heard a shout from the other end of the pool.

"What happened to you?" Matt called. "We were supposed to be racing!"

"I … er … got cramp in my leg…" Joe yelled back. He pretended to rub his calf muscle. "Look," he hissed to Fizz. "You're dead because the other fish decided to have you for breakfast. Now please, leave me alone." He waved to Matt. "Come on, we'd better get changed."

"You can swim, but you can't hide," growled Fizz. "If you won't help me, I'll feed you to the fishes!"

"What?" Joe rolled his eyes. "You're just a goldfish! What can you do?"

But the fish didn't reply. It turned and swam off, vanishing into the deep end.

"How's the cramp?" asked Matt, as they headed for the changing rooms.

"Oh, er … better, thanks."

"I reckon it was just an excuse," said Matt.

"What?" Joe felt his cheeks turn red. Surely Matt hadn't heard him talking to the goldfish?

"Yeah," grinned Matt, "because you knew I was about to beat you – again!"

Joe breathed a sigh of relief.

"At last!" said Dad, who was sitting on the wooden benches in the changing room, rubbing Toby's hair dry with a towel. "Mum will be wondering where we've got to!"

"Sorry," Joe said. He crossed to the lockers that ran down the side of the changing room and grabbed his towel. Then he and Matt headed for the showers.

"Hey, Joe, I don't suppose you're free

tomorrow, are you?" asked Matt. "It's my Uncle Frank's birthday and he's having a barbecue."

Joe groaned inside. He knew exactly where this conversation was going. Matt hated family parties because he always got stuck playing with his younger cousins, Lolly and Lily. He probably wanted Joe to go along with him, to share the awfulness.

"I was wondering if you fancied coming," said Matt.

"Er … I'm not sure," Joe turned on his shower, hoping Matt would drop the subject.

"It'll be fun," Matt continued. "Dan's got some amazing computer games."

Joe made a face. As if Dan would let them play with his stuff! He was sixteen. "Well, I'm not sure what we're doing tomorrow…"

"You're not doing anything, Joe!" called Dad from the changing rooms. "Except tidying your bedroom! A barbecue sounds much more fun!"

UNDEAD PETS

Joe made a face. Dad wasn't helping. "But I haven't finished my homework."

"What homework?" said Matt. "We haven't got any."

"No offence, Matt," said Joe, "but I'm not really keen on your family parties…"

"I'll let you borrow any of my Xbox games," begged Matt.

"No!"

"How about the new footy one? You can have it for a whole week!"

Joe was about to say he wasn't interested even if he got a game for a month, when there was a choking sound and the water stopped. Joe peered up and gave the shower a thump…

POP! The water burst out, along with a small slimy blob that landed on Joe's face.

"Hello, Joe," growled Fizz. "I'm back!"

"Argh!" Joe flicked the fish out of his face. It landed with a splat on the tiled floor.

"Are you ready to help me now?" the fish said, flapping around Joe's toes.

Joe tried to ignore the horrible slimy feeling of the undead fish on his feet.

"I want you to go to Dan's house and find out who killed me. Or else…"

Or else what? thought Joe.

At that moment, Fizz shot off down the plughole. Joe heard an echoing cry rise up from the pipes below. "Don't let me down!"

Matt turned off the shower and grabbed his towel. "So, the barbecue starts at midday. We could pick you up on the way?"

"I'm not sure…" muttered Joe. He flicked off his shower and followed Matt back to the lockers. Dad was already zipping up his swimming bag.

"What's the matter, Joe?" said Dad. "You should be jumping at the chance to go to a party."

Joe didn't answer. He pulled his clothes out of the locker and started to get dressed.

"I wish someone would invite *me* to a barbecue," sighed Dad. "That sounds much more fun than fixing the leaky bathroom tap, which is what I've got to look forward to!"

"Yeah," muttered Joe. "Lucky me!"

They were late to collect Mum. By the time they'd dropped Matt off, she was standing outside the salon where she worked, waiting for them.

"Did you have a good time at the pool?" she asked, as she climbed in to the car.

"Great!" Toby beamed. "I swam underwater!"

"That's brilliant! And what about you, Joe?"

"Oh, yeah, it was good fun," he said unenthusiastically. The truth was, he *had* been having fun, until the crazy zombie fish had showed up and ruined things!

"Joe's been invited to Matt's family barbecue tomorrow," said Dad, as they drove to the supermarket.

"That's nice!"

"I'm not going," said Joe. "I'd just get stuck playing with Lolly and Lily and all Matt's other cousins. The last thing I want is to spend my afternoon babysitting."

UNDEAD PETS

"Well, a barbecue might be fun," said Mum. "Matt's family usually throw great parties."

Joe scowled at the back of his mum's head.

"Can I push the trolley?" Toby asked, as they pulled in to the supermarket car park.

"No!" Mum and Dad said together. Toby treated shopping trolleys like scooters!

"Can I wait in the car?" asked Joe.

"No!" they both answered again.

"Remember that time when you were fiddling with the handbrake," said Dad, "and the car started to roll downhill…"

Joe groaned. "Dad! I was *six* then!"

"Hey!" said Toby. "I'm six!"

But Mum was already opening Joe's door. "Come on – I only need a few things."

You always say that, thought Joe. But as he followed them into the store, he cheered up. At least Fizz couldn't follow him in here. There was no water for a fish to swim in.

"Can you fetch me a jar of pickled onions, Joe?" Mum asked.

He walked through the supermarket, looking for the right aisle… Finally he found them. He was just about to pick up a jar, when something moved inside it.

A beady eye looked out at him. Fizz!

"Hello, Joe!"

He jumped. Fizz was wedged into the jar, glaring out at him.

"Go away!" Joe said, looking round to make sure no one had noticed him talking. But Fizz didn't go away. He began to flip wildly around in the jar, back and forth, faster and faster. The jar started to wobble.

"Stop that!"

But Fizz just did it more.

"I warned you!" growled Fizz. "But you wouldn't listen."

"Watch it!" cried Joe.

Suddenly … SMASH! The jar wobbled right off the shelf.

"No!" gasped Joe. He looked up to see the other shoppers in the aisle giving him stern looks and shaking their heads.

"Fizz?" Joe glanced down to see if the fish was floundering around amongst the pieces of broken glass on the floor. But he'd vanished.

"What's happened here?" said a grumpy voice. A shop assistant, pushing a trolley piled with soup tins, had appeared next to Joe.

"I'm sorry – I was just fetching a jar for my mum, when it slipped through my fingers." He looked at his feet, his cheeks burning.

"Oh," said the woman frostily. "Well, these things happen, I suppose. I'll get a dustpan and brush. Don't touch the glass!"

As she stomped off, Joe spotted another jar wobbling, further along the shelf.

"I'm still here!" rasped Fizz, peering out of it. "Are you ready to help find my killer now?"

"I know who killed you!" said Joe crossly. "It was a bunch of goldfish in your tank – and to be honest, I don't blame them!" He picked up the jar so Fizz couldn't make it fall off the shelf, but when he looked inside, Fizz had gone.

"Over here, Joe!"

He spun round and spotted Fizz swishing around inside a bottle of cooking oil on the other side of the aisle. As Joe watched, the bottle began to wobble.

"No!" Joe yelped. He dived across and caught it just before it fell off the shelf. "Stop doing that!" he snapped.

"Not until you help me find my killer!"

"But I've already told you," said Joe. "You were eaten by your friends!"

"I wasn't!" growled Fizz. "A human killed me!"

"What?"

But just then the shop assistant returned with a set of small cones to mark off the area where the jar had smashed, so she could clean it up. Joe grabbed another jar of pickled onions and raced back to find his parents. As he ran down the aisle, he saw Fizz everywhere he looked. The goldfish seemed to pop up in every jar or bottle that he passed.

"I'm watching you!" said the goldfish, peering out of a jar of French dressing, as Joe hurtled round the corner.

"Here are the onions," panted Joe, dropping the jar in the trolley. He heard a gurgling sound and a growly voice said: "I'm back, Joe!"

Fizz was floating in a bottle of mineral water that his dad had just put in the trolley. Joe groaned.

CHAPTER THREE

Joe kept his eye on Fizz for the rest of the shopping trip, but the fish was quiet, floating in the water bottle and staring silently into space.

"Mmm, chicken curry!" said Dad, as they passed the supermarket café. "Shall we have lunch here?"

Mum checked her watch. "OK, you put the shopping in the car and I'll get in the queue. What do you want for lunch, boys?"

Joe glanced at the hot plate. "Fish and chips, and a banana milkshake, please."

"Me, too," said Toby, who always wanted the same as his big brother.

"OK, boys, go and find a table, I'll be over in a minute."

Joe chose a table by the window. He could see Dad in the car park, loading the bags of shopping into the car. He wondered whether Fizz was still in the bottle.

"Look, Joe!" said Toby proudly. He'd built a tower with the little packets of sugar from the table.

"Great," said Joe, not really concentrating.

"Don't play with the sugar, Toby," said Mum, as she came over carrying a huge tray laden with food. Dad came back in and helped Mum unload the plates onto the table.

"Fish and chips twice and double milkshakes!" Mum handed Joe and Toby their drinks.

"Thanks, Mum."

Joe took a drink of his milkshake. It was delicious – thick and creamy. He blew a few bubbles with his straw. Toby did the same.

"Eat your lunch, please," said Mum with a disapproving face.

Joe took a bite of a chip. "Ow!" he gasped, fanning his mouth. It was burning hot. He grabbed his milkshake and took a huge slurp to put out the fire, and that's when he saw it: a slimy orange face peering out of his drink.

"Hello, Joe…"

"Urgh!" Joe spat out his milkshake.

"Joe!" Mum exclaimed.

"Sorry! My chips are hot!"

He grabbed a sachet of ketchup and spread it on his chips, trying not to look at his drink. But he couldn't help himself. Fizz looked so freaky with his face pressed up against the glass. His single open eye looked even larger and scarier than before.

Joe felt queasy.

Fizz blew a string of green bubbles in the glass and looked at Joe's lunch plate. "I can't believe you're eating fish!" he rasped. "Traitor!" Joe scowled back at him. "Are you ready to help me now, Joe?"

Joe shrugged. He couldn't exactly talk with everyone round him.

Fizz's eyes narrowed. Then he began to flip wildly, making more frothy bubbles float to the top. Joe glanced at his parents. Had they noticed? But they were too busy listening to Toby, who was telling Mum a long story about swimming.

"It's your last chance. Help me or there'll be trouble!" growled Fizz.

Joe made an exasperated face and went to

grab the shaking glass. But just as he reached out, Fizz did an extra big flip and knocked it over completely, splattering milkshake across the table and on to Joe's lap.

"Wow!" giggled Toby, his eyes wide.

"Joe!" Mum jumped up as the milky puddle reached her side of the table.

"Sorry, it was an accident…"

"What's got into you today?" asked Dad, reaching over and picking up the glass.

"You must be more careful," said Mum, soaking up the mess with a wad of napkins. "Look at you, you're soaked!"

Joe stood up. His jeans and T-shirt were covered in milkshake.

"You look like you've peed your pants," giggled Toby.

Joe shot him a scowl. But Toby was right. It did look like that.

As soon as they got home, Joe raced upstairs and stripped off his wet clothes. He put on a clean T-shirt and jeans and then Mum popped her head round the door.

"Give them to me," she said crossly, scooping up the pile of clothes. "I still can't believe you made such a mess in the supermarket, Joe!"

He shrugged. "I told you, I didn't mean to…"

Mum sighed. "I'll add them to the next load of washing."

When she'd gone, Joe lay on his bed, thinking about Fizz. Why did the fish think a human had killed him? For some reason Fizz just didn't seem to want to accept the truth – that he'd been gobbled up by his tank mates! Suddenly Joe had an idea. He jumped off his bed, and went over to his bookcase. He was sure he had a book about goldfish somewhere…

Maybe if I can find proof that fish really do eat each other sometimes, he thought, *then Fizz will believe me and push off into the afterlife!*

He pulled out a thin book with a fancy fan-tailed goldfish on the front and leafed through a few pages. "There!" he said triumphantly, reading a section with the heading "Looking After Your Goldfish".

Looking After Your Goldfish

Goldfish are social creatures who like to live in groups. But if you keep more than one fish, you'll need a big tank. Keeping fish in a tank that is too small can make them stressed and ill. Cannibalism is rare – but it can happen if you don't feed your fish properly.

"Ha!" said Joe. "Proof!"

He was just wondering where to find Fizz so he could show him the book, when suddenly he heard a scream from the kitchen.

CHAPTER FOUR

Joe raced downstairs and found Mum crouching in front of the washing machine, which was churning out soapy water on to the kitchen floor.

"Quick, Joe!" wailed Mum. "Fetch your dad from the garage, before the house floods!"

As Joe turned to go, he saw a flash of orange surfing through the foamy puddle that was forming.

"I told you there'd be trouble if you didn't help me," growled Fizz.

Joe glared at him, then dashed outside to find Dad.

"Hello, Joe. Want to help me wash the car to earn some extra pocket money?"

"Dad! Quick! The washing machine's gone berserk and it's flooding the kitchen!"

Dad groaned. "Not another thing to fix!" He thrust the bucket he was carrying into Joe's hands. "Make a start, would you, Joe? I'll be back soon." He dashed off indoors.

Joe reached into the bucket for the sponge, but instead he felt something wriggle between his fingers… Joe peered into the bucket. "Did you break the washing machine, Fizz?"

"Might have done, can't remember."

Joe dumped the bucket on the ground with a thud. Then he squatted down next to it. "Who do you think you are? The Cod-father!"

"Huh!" rasped the fish. "If you'd done what I asked, it wouldn't have happened. I've told you,

UNDEAD PETS

I can't pass over until you help me!"

"But how? What do you expect me to do?"

"Find out who killed me."

"I keep telling you, the other fish ate you."

"They didn't! They wouldn't dare." Fizz swam around the bucket for a bit. "I was the boss of the tank, you know. The toughest fish! None of the others would have dared eat me."

"Well, maybe Dan forgot to feed them and they got hungry," said Joe. "I've been reading about it – it does happen!"

"Not to me!" snapped the fish. "That isn't what happened!"

"So what did happen, then?"

I was Dan's first fish.

Others came along, but I was always the boss.

One day I was having a quiet doze...

When suddenly a net scooped me up.

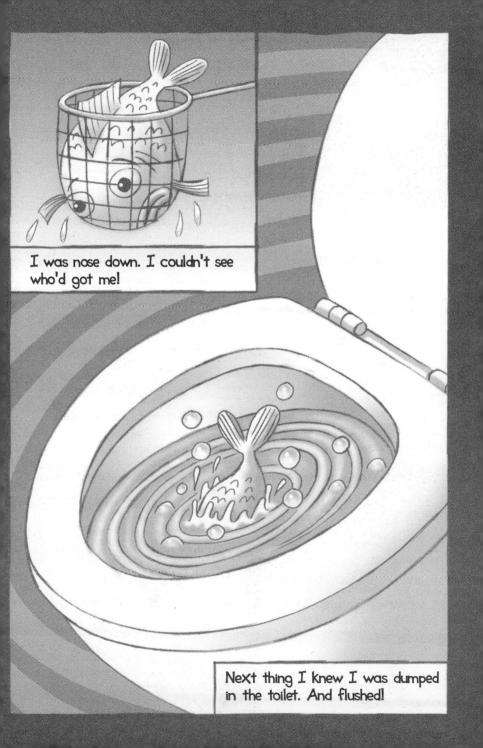

I was nose down. I couldn't see who'd got me!

Next thing I knew I was dumped in the toilet. And flushed!

"You got flushed down the toilet?" said Joe incredulously.

"Yeah!" Fizz made a choking sound.

"So who put you in there?"

"I don't know. I couldn't see!"

"But that's ridiculous!"

Fizz glared up at him. "Have you ever been stuck nose down at the bottom of a fish net? No? Well, trust me, you don't get the best view!"

"OK, OK, calm down! There can't be many suspects," said Joe. "Was it Dan? Maybe he got fed up with you…"

"No chance!" Fizz growled.

"Or his mum and dad? Maybe they didn't like your grumpy face!"

"Ha!"

"Or what about one of Dan's little sisters, then — Lily or Lolly? Matt says they're a real handful."

"I've told you! I don't know who did it and it's your job to find out!"

"Well, give me some clues, at least! Was it a grown-up or a child? I know Matt's got loads of little cousins, so it could have been one of them."

"I told you, I don't know!" yelled Fizz. "Dan doesn't like people going in his room, so I don't know who's who! *You* find out!"

Joe puffed out his cheeks. "How? I'm not Sherlock Holmes!"

"That's your problem," growled the fish. "Go to Dan's house and find out!"

"Oh no!" said Joe, shaking his head firmly. "No way. I am *not* going to that barbecue tomorrow!"

Fizz swished round the bucket, splashing Joe with soapy water. "Then say hello to your new pet," he growled, "cos I'm going nowhere until you find out who killed me!"

For the rest of the day, Fizz hung around like a bad smell. Wherever Joe went, Fizz went, too.

When Joe was watching TV, Fizz materialized in the vase on the mantelpiece, blowing green bubbles and glaring at Joe menacingly. When Joe had a drink, Fizz popped up in the glass. And when Joe went for a wee, Fizz was already there, waiting in the U-bend.

"Go to Dan's!" he boomed up. "Or else!"

"Go away!" Joe hissed. "I can't pee when you're there!"

UNDEAD PETS

Joe was glad when it was bedtime. He reckoned that his bedroom was the one place Fizz couldn't find him. There was no water in there!

"Don't forget to pull out the plug in the sink after you've had a wash," called Dad, as Joe headed upstairs. "I haven't had time to fix that leaky tap yet. We don't want another flood today!"

But Joe wasn't listening. He was thinking about Fizz. Who could have killed him ... and why?

As Joe filled the sink, he expected Fizz to burst out of one of the taps. But he didn't. "Where are you?" Joe whispered. He didn't trust that fish! But there was still no sign of him.

Joe brushed his teeth, then turned off the cold tap as best he could. It was leaking quite badly now. He turned off the bathroom light and headed back to his room.

As he climbed into bed he thought about Fizz being flushed down the toilet and chuckled. He looked forward to telling Uncle Charlie about it when he came for his next visit. *I wonder where he is right now?* thought Joe, as he closed his eyes. *Probably exploring a lost city somewhere…*

Joe was just drifting off, dreaming about a city at the bottom of the sea, when suddenly he heard a yell from the bathroom…

"Joe Edmunds! I told you not to leave the plug in the sink!"

He opened his eyes and sat up. "What?"

Dad's head appeared round Joe's door. He looked furious. "The bathroom floor is soaking, Joe! If I hadn't come up, you'd have flooded the house!"

Undead Pets

Joe rubbed his eyes. "But I didn't leave the plug in."

"Well, someone must have and you were the last person in there. The sink was overflowing when I went in!"

Joe gritted his teeth. Fizz!

Mum came into the room with a glass of water. "Your head's been all over the place today, Joe!" She put the glass by Joe's bed and bent down to kiss him. "Goodnight. Try and be a bit more careful tomorrow, OK!"

"Goodnight, Joe," Dad added.

"Night," Joe replied.

As Mum closed his door, shutting out the light from the landing, Joe spotted a strange glow coming from the water glass.

And then a sarcastic voice said, "Night, night, Joe. Don't let the bed-fish bite!"

It took Joe ages to nod off after that. Fizz didn't say anything else. But knowing that the zombie fish was in his room gave Joe the creeps. Every time he drifted off, he dreamed about shark-sized goldfish chasing him up and down the swimming pool.

"Whoooa!" he yelled, sitting bolt upright, just as another monster fish was about to gobble him up. He glanced at his clock. It was 6 a.m. He felt tired and groggy, and his throat was dry. Without thinking, he reached for his water glass and glugged down a few mouthfuls. The water tasted odd – slightly fishy. And then he remembered why!

"Morning, Joe!"

"Urgh!" Joe spat out the water. "Gross!" He felt like he was about to throw up. "You didn't poo in there, did you?"

"Can't remember," rasped Fizz.

Joe banged down the glass. "OK, OK! I've had enough," he snapped. "You win. I'll call Matt and tell him I'll go to the barbecue. And when I get there I'll try and find out what happened. But I'm not making any promises!"

The fish fixed its beady eye on him. "Smart move, Joe. You're finally beginning to use your brain."

CHAPTER FIVE

Dan and his family lived on the other side of town in a big stone house with a long gravel drive.

"I hope you're hungry, because Uncle Frank loves food!" said Matt. "He's got one of those giant barbecues – it's bigger than our car!"

"Great," said Joe unenthusiastically.

They were in the car. Joe was imagining what was in store when they got to the party – an afternoon playing with the twins ... not to mention having to somehow unmask a fish killer at the same time. He was holding the water bottle he was carrying Fizz in.

"Have they still got the guinea pigs?" Joe asked. He remembered Matt once telling him that the twins had each been given one.

Matt made a grim face. "No. They left the hutch open by mistake and they escaped!"

Lucky guinea pigs, thought Joe gloomily.

"I reckon they planned it," chuckled Matt's dad from the front.

"Yeah," added Matt. "To get away from the twins!"

"That's unfair," scolded his mum. "The girls were devastated. Remember, they're only little."

"Yeah, little monsters!" said Matt's dad under his breath.

"Oh, look, there's Aunt Jane!" said Matt's mum, as they pulled up outside the house.

Joe recognized her from a party at Matt's house last Christmas. She looked just like her

UNDEAD PETS

twin daughters – small, blonde and very girly.

"Hi, Matt! Hi, Joe! I'm really glad you could come," she said, as they climbed out of the car.

Her husband Frank appeared behind her. "Great to see you again, Joe," he beamed.

"Er … yeah, thanks for inviting me."

As Joe followed them through the house and into the back garden, Matt nudged him. "I still can't believe you decided to come."

"Yeah," muttered Joe. "Me neither!"

"Everyone's in the garden," said Uncle Frank. "The barbecue's up and running, so the food won't be long. What do you want to drink, boys — Coke, lemonade?" He noticed the water bottle in Joe's back pocket, where Fizz was hiding. "I see you've come prepared, Joe. You'll need lots of water today — it's going to be a scorcher!"

"Enough chat. Get to work," growled Fizz. "Find my killer!"

Joe sighed. It was going to be a long afternoon!

The back garden was large, and it was already full of people. There were grown-ups wearing floaty dresses and bright shirts, and a gang of small children playing in a sandpit.

Right in the middle were Lolly and Lily, the twins. Both had blonde bunches and matching pink swimsuits.

"Maybe they won't notice us," whispered Matt, trying to hide behind a group of chattering adults.

"Fat chance!" muttered Joe.

"Maaaaattttt!" screeched one of the twins. (Joe could never tell which was which.) "Come and play!"

She charged across the grass towards her favourite older cousin, grabbing his arm and trying to haul him towards the sandpit. "You, too!" She grabbed Joe's arm with her other hand.

"Maybe later," said Matt, wriggling free.

"Oh, you two don't mind playing with the little ones, do you?" said Aunt Jane. "They've been looking forward to seeing you all day."

"Oh, OK," said Matt, looking apologetically at Joe.

The other twin joined her sister, and they both dragged the boys towards the sandpit. "Come and play!"

Joe groaned. There were loads of other little kids there, too!

"That's Martha and Henry," said Matt, nodding to a couple of wild-looking toddlers, who were trying to bury each other in sand. "And that one's Emma." He pointed to a little girl picking her nose. "Billy's the one in the green cap. Watch him, he's a biter! He once tried to eat his nursery hamster — but they rescued it just in time…"

Joe stared at the little boy. If he attacked hamsters, maybe he flushed fish?

"Oh, and that's Franklin over there," said Matt. "He likes to pinch — really hard! So keep your eye on him, too!"

Each of the children seemed worse than the last!

"Play babies — now!" said one of the twins. The little girl dropped a scruffy doll into Joe's lap. It had scribbles on its face and no hair. "Baby needs her nappy changed."

Matt, who was building sandcastles next to him, made another apologetic face.

"Right," said Joe, not sure where to start.

Just then he felt his water bottle twitch and heard Fizz shout, "Come on, Joe! Why aren't you trying to find out who killed me?"

Joe took the water bottle out of his back pocket and pretended to take a swig.

"I am!" he hissed. "Keep calm!" Then he smiled at the kids. "So ... where's Dan?" He glanced around the garden to see if he could spot Matt's oldest cousin.

"In his room," said one of the twins crossly. "He never plays!"

"Lucky him," muttered Joe.

"Well, maybe he thinks he's a bit big to play,"

said Matt pointedly. "He's sixteen now."

"Change baby's nappy!" said the other twin, poking Joe.

"OK, Lily." Joe sighed, peeling off the doll's nappy.

"I'm Lolly!" The little girl scowled.

Meanwhile, Fizz was getting more and more agitated in Joe's water bottle. "Ask them who killed me!" growled the fish. "Come on, Joe, do something!"

But before he could say anything, Lolly grabbed his hand. "Baby wants a bath!" She dragged him across to the paddling pool. "Fill it up!" she demanded, pointing to a garden hose.

"Ow!" Joe felt something sharp prick his hand. He looked down. Billy was standing there.

"Did you just bite me?" said Joe, rubbing his hand. Then he felt a pinch on his left leg. "Hey!"

"Fill the pool!" said the pincher.

"All right, all right…" Joe glared at them both. "Matt, is it OK to put some water in the paddling pool?"

"I think so. Not too much."

Joe turned on the hose and the water splashed into the pool. The children climbed in.

Suddenly, Fizz appeared in amongst them, gliding around like a grumpy shark.

Joe glared at him. That was all he needed!

One of the twins had found a bucket full of toys and was tipping them into the pool. Rubber ducks and plastic fish bobbed about in the water.

Joe turned off the hose and picked one up. "How about we play catch the goldfish?"

The children squealed, and made a dive for the floating fish.

"So, do these fish look like the ones in Dan's room?" asked Joe, hoping to catch a guilty look on someone's face.

Lily frowned. "Don't know. We're not allowed in Dan's room."

"What about you ... er ... Billy?" Joe asked the hand-biter. "Do you sometimes go and look at Dan's goldfish?"

The little boy stuck his tongue out at Joe.

"Great," Joe muttered. Then he bent down to speak to Fizz (pretending to fiddle with the hose, so no one would notice). "Are you sure you don't remember anything about the person who flushed you? What about the hand that held the net? Was it big or small?"

"I told you, I couldn't see anything!" growled the fish.

Joe groaned. How was he supposed to crack this case when his only witness was an undead goldfish?

"Hey, lads – want something to eat?" Uncle Frank came over carrying two serving dishes. "Fresh off the barbecue! We've got bangers, burgers and loads of fish…"

"What?" Fizz said. "Did he say fish?"

"I've got tiger prawns, sardines, mackerel…" said Uncle Frank proudly.

"Monster!" growled Fizz. And then suddenly he disappeared.

"More water!" wailed Lily.

Joe turned on the hose, but nothing came out. He peered inside, then gave it a shake, but *still* no water came out. "Something must be jamming it," he said.

Uncle Frank, meanwhile, was still waffling on about his favourite fish to barbecue. "Look at those prawns – don't they look juicy! Go on, Joe, try one…"

Suddenly there was a loud POP! and Fizz burst out of the pipe, along with all the water that had built up behind him.

SKOOSH!!!!!!!! The hose whipped out of control, spraying water over all of them.

"Hey!" yelped Uncle Frank, trying to shield the food.

"Sorry, sorry!" said Joe, wrestling wildly with the twitching hose.

"Joe funny!" giggled Lolly.

"Daddy all wet," laughed Lily.

And then all the children joined in – belly laughing hysterically and pointing at Uncle Frank and his soaking wet shirt.

CHAPTER SIX

"It serves him right," said Fizz sulkily. "The man's a monster!"

"You shouldn't have done it!" whispered Joe. "He thought it was me messing about with the hose. If you cause too much trouble I won't get to stay – then I won't be able to find your killer!"

They were talking in the toilet, out of the way of all the party guests.

"Are you sure you didn't recognize any of the children?" asked Joe.

"No! I told you, I didn't see who flushed me."

"Then how can I help you?"

"That's your problem!"

There was a rattle on the door. "Hurry up, Joe!" called Matt. "I'm bursting!"

"Look, we've got to go. Remember, no more silly stuff, OK?"

"Huh!" growled the fish, as Joe flushed the toilet.

As soon as he opened the door, Matt rushed in. "Wait there for me, then we'll go down and get a hot dog."

"Or maybe some barbecued fish!" said Joe.

"I heard that," growled Fizz.

Joe heard a shout…

"There he is!"

He turned to see the twins, and the rest of their gang, thundering up the stairs towards him.

"Joe, play with us *now!*" grinned Lily.

"What? Er … no…"

"Come and see my dollies," said Lolly, taking Joe's hand. The kids dragged and pushed him down the corridor, into the twins' bedroom.

Joe blinked at the bright pink wallpaper. The curtains were pink, too. So was the carpet. And the two little beds had matching pink duvet covers, with white stars.

"It's very … er…"

"Pink?" chuckled Matt, appearing in the doorway.

"Hello, Matt!" beamed Lolly. "This is my new doll. Her name's Rose. Let's have a tea party…"

Joe felt his water bottle moving again. Fizz was back. But Joe had noticed something else – a book lying next to one of the beds. It had a smiling goldfish on the front: *Little Bubble's Big Adventure.*

He was about to pick it up and take a look
when Lily suddenly grabbed his hand.

"Let's play hide-and-seek!"

"What? OK." That sounded slightly better
than dolls' tea parties! "Right, me and Matt will
count to twenty," said Joe. "You lot hide. Ready?
One, two, three, four, five, six…"

He waited until the children had disappeared out of the room, then he stopped counting and collapsed on the bed. "Blimey," he said. "I thought Toby was hard work!"

Matt smiled sheepishly. "Yeah, they're really full on. You can see why Dan stays in his room a lot."

"Where is his room, anyway?"

"Down the hall."

"Can we go and see him? I'd love to get a look at his killer fish!" said Joe.

"Huh!" muttered Fizz. "That lot couldn't kill a water flea!"

Joe ignored Fizz and said to Matt, "Come on, let's give it a try!"

Matt looked doubtful. "He might not let us."

Joe eventually persuaded Matt. They went to Dan's room and banged on the door.

"Go away!" came the answer.

"Dan? It's me, Matt…"

"Go *away*!"

Matt sighed. "See!"

"Tell him I want to see his fish, because I'm thinking of getting some."

Matt shrugged. "Hey, Dan, my mate Joe's here. He wants to see your fish tank — he's thinking of getting one of his own."

There was silence for a few minutes, then the door opened a crack and Dan peered out. He was tall with shaggy black hair and a grumpy expression.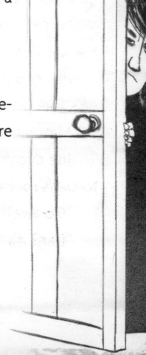

"Are the twins with you?"

Matt shook his head.

"They think we're playing hide-and-seek." Joe grinned. "They're hiding, but we're not seeking!"

Dan smiled and opened the door a bit more. "Get in, before they hear you."

The room was dark — the curtains were pulled shut and the only lights were from a TV, with a game on pause, and a large illuminated fish tank.

"Wow!" Joe breathed, as he and Matt examined a detailed model of a spaceship.

Matt reached out to pick it up.

"Don't touch anything!" hissed Dan, pushing his long fringe out of his eyes.

"Sorry…" said Matt.

There were more models dotted around the room, along with piles of computer games. In the corner was an electric guitar and a dusty black amp. The walls were covered with movie and music posters, books and DVDs were piled on the bookcase, and a whole bunch of weird ornaments — a glowing skeleton, a green lava lamp and a road sign saying NO EXIT were scattered around the shelves.

"Wow!" said Joe. "I really like your room."

UNDEAD PETS

The fish tank stood in the corner, glowing like an alien sea world. Joe peered in. There were several small goldfish swimming around, as well as a guppy. Two water snails were stuck to the glass. On the bottom was a model of a shipwreck, and a small skull blowing air bubbles from its mouth.

"Your tank is awesome," said Joe.

Dan bent down and looked in, too. "Yeah, the fish are cool. I used to have a goldfish called Fizz. I'd had him since I was nine. But he got eaten."

"I didn't!" growled Fizz, who had appeared inside the tank. He was floating about the place like a sergeant major carrying out an inspection.

"It was weird that he got killed," Dan continued. "He was always the boss of the tank. I thought he was hard as nails."

"I am!" said Fizz hotly. He peered out of the tank at Dan's room. "I liked it here," he added miserably. "There was lots of stuff to look at. I used to watch TV with Dan – gangster films, monster movies, *Jaws*!"

"Hey, Dan, tell Joe what happened to Fizz," said Matt.

"Well, I was away for a couple of days, camping with a mate. When I got home, Fizz was gone. One of the others had eaten him."

"Rubbish!" growled Fizz.

"Do you know which fish did it?" asked Joe. "I mean, which fish is the cannibal?"

THUD! Fizz banged his head against the glass in frustration. "I keep telling you, they're not cannibals!"

Dan shrugged. "Nope. I've been watching the

tank, but I haven't seen anything."

"Tell him what really happened, Joe," yelled Fizz, pressing right up against the glass of the tank. "Come on! Now's your chance!"

But before Joe could say anything, there was a sudden hammering on the door.

"Matt? Joe? Where are you?"

"The twins," groaned Matt.

"You'll have to go," said Dan. "They're not allowed in here."

But it was too late. Lolly and Lily burst in, followed by the others.

"We found you!" squeaked Lolly. "We've been hiding for ages!"

"But you didn't come and look for us!" added Lily, with a scowl.

"Everyone out!" shouted Dan, as Henry picked up one of his models. "Hey — stop that!" he yelled at Franklin, who was pulling the strings on his guitar. Meanwhile, Billy and Emma had moved over to the fish tank. Emma was pulling faces at the fish, while Billy banged on the glass to scare them.

Joe looked at them both. Was one of them the killer? Joe could imagine Billy flushing a fish just for the fun of it.

"All of you GET OUT!" Dan yelled.

As he headed for the door, Joe spotted a laptop on Dan's desk. There was a webcam on top, which gave Joe an idea...

CHAPTER SEVEN

"Come and play on the slide!" said Lily, grabbing Joe's hand and pulling him downstairs.

Joe was thinking about something else as he was dragged back out into the garden. If he could somehow stake out Dan's room using his webcam, then perhaps he could catch the fish killer in the act! He'd have to set a trap to tempt the killer to strike again… But Joe was sure he could think of some way to make that happen. All he had to do was persuade Dan to let them use the webcam without making him and Matt suspicious!

"Your turn on the slide!" said Lily, pushing Joe forward.

"I think I'm too big…" The slide was pink and plastic and barely came up to Joe's waist.

"Here," said Matt, handing Joe a paper plate with a hot dog on it. "Come and grab a seat."

They sneaked away before the little kids could stop them.

Two smiley aunts made room for them at a table on the lawn. One had curly blonde hair and a dress with red cherries on it. The other wore purple-rimmed glasses, large hooped earrings and lots of jangly bangles.

"Joe, this is Aunt Sal and Aunt Tracey," said Matt.

"Would you like some fruit punch?" asked Aunt Tracey. "It's delicious!" A giant plastic jug in the middle of the table was filled with strawberries, cherries, and slices of lemon and lime, all bobbing about in lemonade.

"Yes, please," said Matt.

"Thanks, that would be great," said Joe.

Aunt Tracey poured them all a glass. And that was when Fizz reappeared – in Aunt Sal's glass!

The fish glared out at Joe. "What are you doing? You shouldn't be sitting around. Have you forgotten what you're here for?"

Joe frowned. He wished he could tell Fizz his stake-out plan for using the webcam to catch the fish killer in the act. But he couldn't – not with people listening.

"So, Joe," said Aunt Sal. "Do you have any hobbies?" She had picked up her glass now, and was holding it in one hand, swirling the ice and fruit – and goldfish! – around.

"Er, well…" Joe stuttered. He couldn't stop staring at her glass. "I like football…"

"Oh, I love sport, too," said Aunt Sal, giving her glass another swirl.

Fizz clunked his head on an ice cube, then exploded at Joe: "So … you've given up! You won't help me, eh? Gone off the idea, have you? Well, watch this…"

Joe watched in horror as a long string of fish poo appeared in Aunt Sal's glass.

"Have you any other interests, Joe?" asked Aunt Tracey, taking a sip from her glass.

"He's nuts about animals," said Matt.

"Really? Me, too!" Aunt Sal smiled. "I'm especially fond of parrots. What about you, Joe? What are your favourite animals?"

But Joe couldn't speak. His eyes were fixed on Aunt Sal's glass. *Please don't drink it*, he thought.

"Joe's interested in all sorts of animals," said Matt pointedly. Joe knew that Matt had been getting a bit fed up with his odd behaviour, which was all down to the undead pets – although Matt didn't know that! "He likes hamsters, cats, dogs … and fish, too," Matt added. "We've just been looking at Dan's goldfish."

"Oh, I heard about them. Turned cannibal, haven't they!" said Aunt Sal. Then she went to take a drink.

"No!" yelped Joe. "There's something in your glass – I think it's a fly!"

"What?" Aunt Sal peered into her tumbler. "I don't see anything."

"Can I have a look?" Joe took the drink from her and glared at Fizz, who was still swishing about inside the glass. "Yeah, there it is," he said. "Shall I pour it away for you?"

Before Aunt Sal could answer, Joe emptied the glass into a nearby plant pot. Fizz instantly vanished, reappearing seconds later in Aunt Tracey's glass.

"Shall I poo in here, too?" he asked menacingly. "I will unless you get back to looking for my killer!"

"Look!" said Joe. "There's Dan!" And as Matt and the aunts turned to look, Joe switched drinks with Aunt Tracey, so he now had the fish glass.

"Very clever," growled Fizz. "But I can play this game all day!"

And he instantly vanished out of the glass in Joe's hand and reappeared inside Matt's drink.

Joe wished a zombie cat would appear and gobble Fizz up! That would fix him!

"Dan, over here!" called Aunt Sal, giving her nephew a wave.

Dan came over with an enormous plate of food, and sat down next to Joe.

"We haven't seen much of you today," said Aunt Tracey.

Dan shrugged moodily, taking a bite of his burger.

Joe turned to Dan. "Hey, Dan, I was thinking… If you want to find out which fish in the tank is the cannibal, maybe we could organize a stake-out…"

"What do you mean?"

"Well, how about we set up your webcam and point it at the fish tank, to monitor it."

"Waste of time," muttered Dan. "I've been watching them for days and nothing's happened. And anyway, I'm going out with my mates soon."

"Well, me and Matt could do it. We wouldn't even have to go in your room. The camera's wireless, isn't it? We could take the laptop somewhere else and watch the fish tank from there…"

"What are you talking about?" said Matt, who'd been chatting to one of his aunts.

"I was just saying we could spy on Dan's fish for him," explained Joe. "Using his webcam and his laptop – so we can spot the killer fish."

"I'm in!" Matt grinned. "We'd be like a real surveillance team."

Dan didn't look keen. "I dunno … I don't like people messing with my stuff."

Then Joe had a brainwave. "Well, it would also be a great way to make sure no one goes into your room…"

"What do you mean?"

"Well, if we set up the camera in the right place we would also be able to see if anyone comes into your room."

Just at that moment, there was a loud wail from the sandpit.

"Looks like Franklin's hit Billy with the spade again!" said Aunt Sal.

Aunt Tracey sighed. "They're such monkeys, those two!"

Matt looked at Dan. "Do you want those kids messing with your stuff?"

"OK, OK," Dan said. "Come upstairs and I'll show you how it works."

"Good plan!" came a fishy voice from Matt's glass. "That's more like it!"

CHAPTER EIGHT

"This is how you turn on the camera. It's got a microphone built in, so you'll be able to hear if anyone sneaks inside. And this is how you see the picture on the laptop…"

"Wow! This is a good camera," said Joe, looking closely at the fish tank.

Dan nodded. "You can take the laptop into any room you like – but be careful with it," he added, handing it over reluctantly. "And don't take it into the bathroom, obviously. I had to save for ages to buy that thing! If anything happens to it, you're dog food!"

Joe swallowed hard. He definitely didn't want to get on the wrong side of Dan.

"Nothing's happening," sighed Matt, peering at the laptop screen.

They were sitting in the twins' bedroom. They'd started off in Jane and Frank's bedroom, but Aunt Jane had chased them out when she'd appeared to reapply her lipstick. Then they'd tried the guest room, but Matt's granddad was already in there having a nap. So that only left the twins' room. They'd been watching the screen for ten minutes, and so far none of the fish had done anything remotely interesting.

Matt puffed out his cheeks. "I don't know why people have fish. They're so boring!"

But Joe was grappling with another problem. He still hadn't thought of a way to tempt the fish killer to strike again. He was pretty sure it was one of the kids. But unless he could get them to do it again, the stake-out was a complete waste of time.

Joe stared at the screen as a fish swam across the tank and glared into the camera. It was Fizz. Joe sighed. He was running out of time. Matt's parents had promised to drop him home by six and it was already five o'clock.

"There's so much stuff in here!" said Matt, knocking over a row of teddies that were arranged on one of the beds.

There were baskets full of toys, a large box filled with dressing-up clothes, a giant set of drawers groaning with paper and pens and sparkly stickers…

"Sarah's room looked a bit like this when we were little," grinned Joe. "It's horrible!" He looked at the kitten-shaped lampshade and the two pairs of fluffy puppy slippers poking out from under the beds. It was truly gruesome!

"Sleeping in here would give me a headache!" groaned Matt. "It's like being trapped inside a stick of candyfloss."

Just then there was a shout from downstairs. "Maaaattttt!"

"Oh no!" he groaned. "They've found us! Quick, Joe, hide the laptop."

Joe shoved it under Lolly's bed, just as they

thundered into the room.

Billy was at the front. He'd found a pirate hat from somewhere and a pointy plastic cutlass, which he waved at Joe. "Give me your treasure or I'll make you walk the plank!"

"Yeah, yeah, very funny," said Matt. "Why don't you all go back and play in the sandpit again."

Billy's answer was to turn his cutlass on Matt and bare his teeth.

"My dolly needs another bath," said Lily, plopping her scribble-faced baby into Joe's lap.

"And I need a wee…" added Lolly.

"Give me your treasure or I'll make you walk the plank!" said Billy again, even louder this time, poking Matt with the cutlass.

"Hey!" said Matt, batting it away. "I haven't got any treasure!" Then a sly smile spread across his face. "How about a real treasure hunt, though?" he said.

"What?" Joe frowned. The last thing he wanted to do was join in another little kids' game. "But, Matt," he whispered. "We can't play games — we're supposed to be doing the stake-out, remember?"

"Don't worry," Matt whispered back. "We won't have to do anything! But this lot will — somewhere else!"

Joe grinned. He understood Matt's idea.

"What sort of treasure hunt?" asked Billy,

giving his cousin another poke with the cutlass.

Matt shrugged. "You have to go and see how many things you can find that start with the letter 'P'."

The kids looked at him blankly.

"'P' for pirate hat!" added Matt, grabbing Billy's hat off his head.

"Hey!" he growled. "Give that back!"

"Or this," said Joe, picking up a pink fluffy pig that was lying on Lolly's bed.

"Or this?" shouted Lolly, holding up her pink pyjamas.

"Exactly!" said Matt.

Then suddenly Joe had another idea. A brilliant idea. An idea that could possibly trap a fish killer!

"'P' is too easy," he said. "Let's choose a different letter. How about 'F'."

"I like 'P' better," wailed Lily. "'P' for pink."

"No!" said Joe firmly. "The letter is 'F.'"

"F for fork," said Matt. "And face paints and … false teeth!"

"And fangs," said Billy.

"Great!" said Joe. "That's brilliant, Billy. But there's loads more stuff that starts with the letter 'F', too – things like flannel, flower, films … and FISH net and FISH food!" he said, looking round to see if any of the children looked especially interested in the word fish! But no one seemed to have noticed…

UNDEAD PETS

For a second, all the kids looked at each other and then there was pandemonium. They were racing and chasing round the room searching for stuff beginning with 'F'.

"Hey!" shouted Matt, fighting to be heard over the din. "You get extra points if you find stuff in other rooms!"

"Downstairs!" yelled Lily, and the kids stampeded out of the room like a herd of wildebeest.

CHAPTER NINE

"I'm not sure that game was such a great idea," sighed Matt, as he flipped open Dan's laptop. "All the kids will probably head straight for Dan's room to rummage round for stuff."

Joe shrugged. "They all went downstairs. Look – there's absolutely nothing happening in Dan's room."

"Yeah," said Matt glumly. "I wish there was though… None of those fish look the slightest bit hungry!"

Joe sat down on one of the beds. As he did,

he spotted the picture book again – the one with the smiley fish on the front.

"*Little Bubble's Big Adventure,*" he read out loud. He reached for it and turned a few pages. "Little Bubble liked to go on adventures…"

Matt grinned. "What's this? Story time with Joe Edmunds? It's not my bedtime, you know."

Joe ignored him and carried on reading. "When Maisie was cleaning out the fish bowl, Little Bubble would jump into the sink and disappear down the plughole, looking for excitement…"

"Yeah, yeah, very nice, Joe!"

"One day, Little Bubble went down the pipes on an amazing underground adventure, all the way to mermaid land…"

"Enough, Joe," Matt groaned.

But Joe didn't need Matt to tell him – he had read enough. He now had a pretty good idea why Fizz had ended up down the toilet. All he had to do was catch the culprit red-handed.

Suddenly, Matt gave a shout. "There's someone in there!"

Joe crouched down to get a better look at the screen. A little girl had appeared in the room. Fizz was going crazy, swimming round in circles.

"Hello, Little Bubble," she said. "I'm looking for things beginning with 'F'. Can you help me?"

"It's one of the twins!" whispered Matt.

"Which one?"

Matt peered closer. "I can't tell. We should go and get her out of Dan's room."

"No," said Joe. "Wait a minute. Let's see what she does…"

They watched as she picked up the fish food. Then she got a hold of the fish net. She looked like she was about to leave, when suddenly she twisted back to look in the tank.

"Little Bubble want to go on another adventure?" she asked with a smile.

"What's she talking about?" whispered Matt. "Oh no! Surely she doesn't think that silly story is for real..."

Fizz was flapping round the tank, shouting, "It was her! It was her! Murderer!"

"Come on, Little Bubble, Lolly take you for another adventure."

Matt's mouth opened in horror. "No!" he shouted. But Lolly had already flipped open the lid of the tank and lowered the net into the water.

"Come on, Little Bubble…"

"Quick!" shouted Joe. "Stop her!"

The boys raced down the corridor, just in time to see Lolly leaving Dan's room and heading to the bathroom, clutching the little fish net in her hand.

"Stop!" yelled Matt.

Lolly turned round. "Little Bubble is going on an adventure to mermaid land."

Joe bent down and tried to take the net from her.

"No, Joe!" she scowled, holding it firmly against her chest.

"Come on," said Joe. "Hand it over!"

Lolly shook her head and held the net tighter.

"Please! Give it to me!" Joe yelped.

"Let go, Lolly," said Matt sternly. He stepped towards her and held out his hand. "Give it to me, now!"

Lolly made a face, then reluctantly handed the net over. Inside was a gasping goldfish.

"Quick, Joe, put it back in the tank."

As Joe headed back to Dan's room, he heard Lolly wail. "Give me Bubble back!"

"At least he's still breathing," growled Fizz, as Joe put the fish carefully back in the tank, "unlike *me*!"

When Joe returned to the landing, he found Matt crouched down in front of Lolly.

"Dan's going to be so mad at you!"

"What's going on here?" It was Aunt Jane — Lolly's mum. "All my forks have gone missing," she said in an angry voice, "and half my flower bed's been chopped to pieces. And your Uncle Sid says his false teeth have been stolen! Do you boys know anything about it?"

UNDEAD PETS

Joe looked at his shoes. Matt bit his lip. "Sorry, Aunt Jane," he muttered. "We were doing a treasure hunt for the kids and we got them to look for things beginning with 'F'."

"Fish food!" beamed Lolly, showing the little box she'd picked up in Dan's room.

"Have you been inside your brother's bedroom again?" said her mum sternly.

Lolly nodded. "And I wanted Bubble to go on another adventure…"

"Pardon?"

Matt sighed. "It was Lolly who killed Dan's fish," he said. "She wanted the goldfish to have adventures like the ones in her book, *Little Bubble's Big Adventure*, so she flushed it down the toilet. She was just about to do the same to another one when we stopped her. "

"Oh, Lolly," said her mum. "Goldfish can't really go off on adventures. They die if you put them down the loo."

The little girl looked at Matt, and then at her mum. Her lip began to wobble and she burst into tears.

"I'll just go and check on the fish," said Joe.

CHAPTER TEN

"Ha!" Fizz growled from inside the tank. "The murderer has been unmasked!"

Joe scowled at the fish. "Well, at least the rest of the tank is safe now. Lolly won't be flushing away any of the others."

"Lucky them!" snapped Fizz. He swam round the tank for a bit, glaring at the other fish, then he stopped and stared out at Joe. "I think it's time I was going. Now I know who killed me, I feel sort of … peaceful."

"Oh … right…" Joe tried to hide his relief.

He definitely wouldn't miss Fizz!

"Bye, Joe."

And he vanished.

Just then, Joe heard a noise at the door.

"Who were you talking to?" Matt was standing in the doorway with a suspicious look on his face. "Were you just talking to the fish tank?"

"Oh, yeah. I ... really like the guppy."

"Well, hopefully now it'll be safe from the

phantom fish killer!" Matt said. "Though Dan's going to be cross with Lolly when he finds out what really happened."

There was a shout from downstairs. "Matt! Joe! We're leaving now!"

"I suppose I'd better go and turn off the webcam," said Matt. "It's still recording!"

"What?" Joe turned pale.

"Yeah – Dan put the camera on record, in case we wanted to take a break."

"So it's recording everything I've been saying in here?" said Joe nervously.

Matt nodded.

"I'll go and turn it off!" said Joe, dodging past his friend. *And I'd better delete everything it's recorded, too!* he thought.

Matt's parents were already in the car by the time they got downstairs.

"Thanks for coming, boys," said Uncle Frank. Lolly, who was holding his hand, gave them a sulky scowl.

"I hope you enjoyed yourselves," said Aunt Jane, who was carrying three forks and a face flannel in her hands. "You've certainly kept the little ones amused!"

Matt grinned, and Joe tried not to laugh.

"Thanks, Aunt Jane," said Matt.

"Yeah, it was great!" added Joe. It was definitely good to have got rid of Fizz, at least.

As Joe followed Matt to the car, something white and fluffy hopped past him and disappeared into the bushes.

"What was that?" Joe gasped.

"Mmm?" Matt peered out of the back seat. "I didn't see anything."

Joe crouched down and peeped into the bushes, but whatever it was had gone. Joe was just about to go, when he noticed something odd on the ground. It was a trail of tiny green balls. Joe frowned. They looked rather like…

"Rabbit poo?"

OUT NOW!

MEET the characters!

ENTER the competition!

www.undeadpets.co.uk

WATCH the trailer!

PLAY the game!

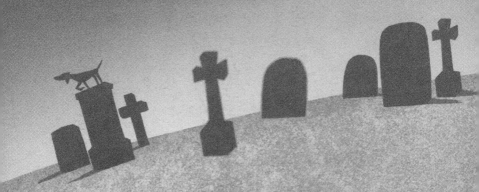